To my loved ones
—Selma

E
387-3042

Translation copyright © 2009 by Editions Auzou.

All rights reserved. Published in the United States by Golden Books, an imprint of Random House Children's Books, a division of Random House, Inc., 1745 Broadway, New York, NY 10019. Originally published in France as *Bisous Bisous*, copyright © 2008 by Editions Philippe Auzou, Paris. Golden Books, A Golden Book, and the G colophon are registered trademarks of Random House, Inc.

Visit us on the Web!
www.randomhouse.com/kids
Educators and librarians, for a variety of teaching tools, visit us at www.randomhouse.com/teachers

Library of Congress Control Number: 2009924796
ISBN: 978-0-375-86431-5 (trade) — ISBN: 978-0-375-96431-2 (lib. bdg.)
MANUFACTURED IN CHINA
10 9 8 7 6 5 4 3 2 1

Kiss Kiss

Written and illustrated by Selma Mandine
Translated by Michelle Williams

g A GOLDEN BOOK • NEW YORK

What's a kiss like?

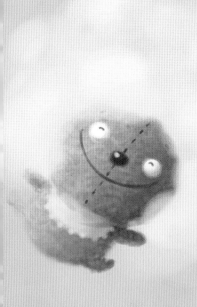

A kiss is supersoft, like cuddly wool.

But sometimes, just like a cactus, it prickles. . . .

Does it hurt?

No, not at all. On the contrary— it tickles!

My grandpa's kiss doesn't prickle.
It's just like cotton candy.
It's all over my face, and then . . .

I can't see a thing when we're cheek to cheek.

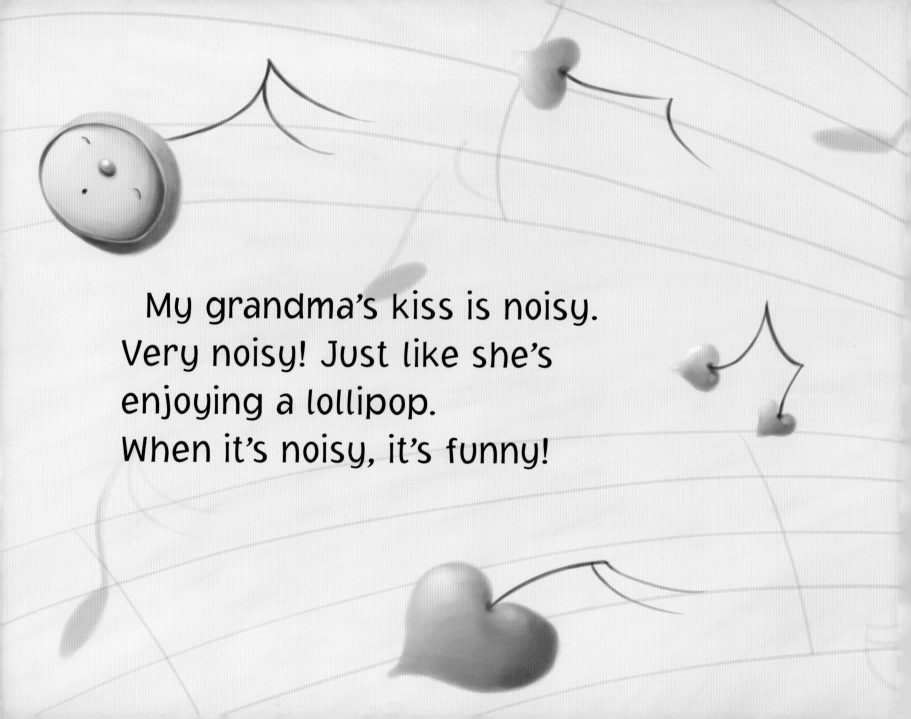

My grandma's kiss is noisy.
Very noisy! Just like she's
enjoying a lollipop.
When it's noisy, it's funny!

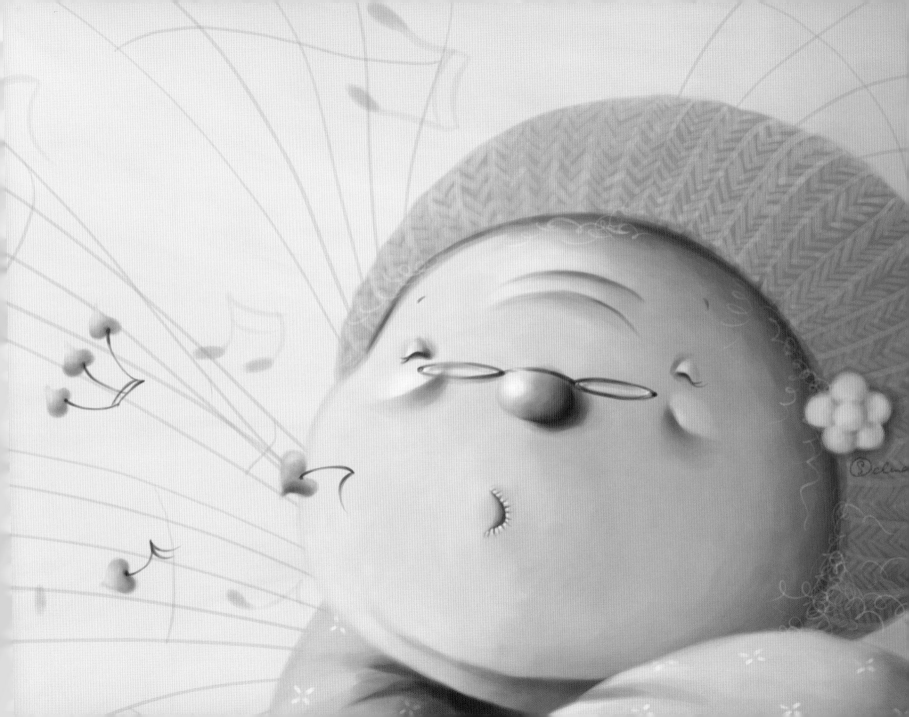

Are there any that we can see?

Of course! Christopher's kisses are always made of chocolate. He always forgets to wipe his mouth.
Mmm! They're tasty!

There are some kisses that are even
sweeter than chocolate or candy. . . .

But they always make me blush.

Sometimes there are also wet ones. . . .

Whose kisses are those?

They're Rex's!

Everybody gives you lots of kisses.

Yes, because everybody loves me.
I get plenty of kisses from everyone!

Now do you understand what
a kiss is?
There are many kinds of kisses,
and they're all different. A kiss is
really wonderful!

Sorry, but I still don't understand exactly what a kiss is.

Oh! Well, here's one. . . .

Hmmmm, it's soft and warm and fresh . . .
It's delicious!
Can you give me a lot more?

Of course I can. I love you. . . .